BECOMING JOE DIMAGGIO

BECOMING
JOE DiMAGGIO

Maria Testa

WITH ILLUSTRATIONS BY
Scott Hunt

CANDLEWICK PRESS
CAMBRIDGE, MASSACHUSETTS

This book was made possible, in part,
by a grant from the Society of Children's Book Writers
and Illustrators.

First edition 2002

Library of Congress Cataloging-in-Publication Data

Testa, Maria.
Becoming Joe DiMaggio / Maria Testa ; illustrated by Scott Hunt. —1st ed.
p.   cm.
ISBN 0-7636-1537-4
1. Italian Americans—Juvenile poetry. 2. Grandfathers—Juvenile poetry.
3. Children's poetry, American. [1. Italian Americans—Poetry.
2. Grandfathers—Poetry. 3. American poetry.]
I. Hunt, Scott (Scott W.), ill. II. Title.
PS3570.E847 B43 2002
811'.54—dc21   2001025886

2 4 6 8 10 9 7 5 3 1

Printed in the United States of America

This book was typeset in Amasis and Quicksans Accurate.
The illustrations were done in charcoal and pastel.

Candlewick Press
2067 Massachusetts Avenue
Cambridge, Massachusetts 02140

visit us at www.candlewick.com

For my brother, Richard,
in memory of our father, Richard L. Testa, M. D.,
and in honor of Joseph Paul DiMaggio

Contents

BECOMING JOE DIMAGGIO

DREAMS 1936

On the day I was born
Papa-Angelo made a chair,
a small chair
a chair for a child
a chair for me.

He sanded it smooth
and polished it with
an oily rag
until it shone so brightly
it astonished him
and made him
smile.

He carried the chair
into the old wooden shed,
the one that still leans
like Pisa

in the middle of the garden
out back, next to the
vacant lot
where everyone on the street
throws junk.

He placed my chair
alongside his chair,
a chair for an old man
with a cushion tied to the back,
a big chair
always facing
the radio on
the rough, round table
in the center of
the shed.

Papa-Angelo had a new grandson,
and the Yankees had
a new center fielder
whose name sounded like music,
and I had a new chair
before I had a name at all.

For the first time
in a long time
Papa-Angelo had dreams
to go with his nightmares.

BAPTISM

Mama likes to tell the story of my
baptism,
likes to tell everyone how
she had no idea what
my name
would be, even when
everyone was standing in the church.

I should have been Alfonso
by right.
The first son
after three beautiful daughters
should always be named for
the father
wherever he may be.

But Mama opened her mouth,
she likes to say,
and no sound came out
so Papa-Angelo leaned closer and
whispered

and then Mama nodded
and smiled
as if her prayers
had finally been
answered.

"Joseph Paul," Mama said out loud,
loving the name from
the beginning,
accepting the promise.

SISTERS

They were already
part of the world when
I came along,
already knew their
roles
and how to play them.

For a long time
it was simple:
one sister to play
mama
when Mama could not,
one sister to play
horse
when my cowboy was stranded,
and one sister to make me
laugh
when no one else
was laughing.

They knew the steps
and they knew the rules,
dancing through every day,
hopes and wishes
rising and falling and sometimes
rising again,
all around
this boy's world.

THE SECOND GIFT

The first gift
was the chair
and I grew into it
quickly,
climbing on the seat
then on the back
standing
　　　jumping
　　　　　flying.

Papa-Angelo gave up on
the lesson of
sitting still then,
knowing that
the day would come
when I would sit
quietly
in that chair,
not moving
and maybe not even
breathing,

only listening to a 3–2 count
with the bases loaded—
the second gift.

CONVERSATION

The police came
and took Papa
away, I said.
          I know.
Papa said
it would just be for
a short time
and the policemen
laughed
and Mama cried.
          I know.
We were supposed
to play catch.
          I know.

The radio was on
of course,
but low.

I stood up
out of my chair,
and climbed into
Papa-Angelo's lap.
I listened to
my grandfather's heart,
beating
strong and steady
and loud,
loud enough
to be heard above
the sudden music of
a Joe DiMaggio
home run.

I love him, you know.
I know.

THE FIRST TIME

I guess Papa-Angelo
got tired of watching
me use garden stakes
and tomatoes
to hit my home runs
or maybe he got tired
of the waste
and the mess.

Here, he said one afternoon
before the game began
and we were still listening
to Caruso sing.

I took the hard white ball
with red stitching
and the smooth wood bat,
and cradled them in my lap
for the rest of the opera
and through the entire game.

I tightened my grip
on the bat
every time Joe DiMaggio
stepped up to the plate.

It worked.
Joe D. went 4 for 4
and drove in the winning run.

For the first time,
I dreamed it was me.

THE WORD

I'd heard the word
so many times before:
when the politicians talk about people
who live on the wrong side
of the law,
when the bosses talk about people
who come in late to work
and can't be trusted
alone in the shop,
when the teachers talk about
the wild boys
who fight on the playground
and throw spitballs
in class,
when the FBI men on newsreels
at the Saturday matinee
talk about people
who "forget" to pay their taxes
of all things,

and especially when the freckle-faced
nephews
of the parish priest
talk about me.

Dago.
I'd heard the word
so many times before
but never felt like screaming
until I heard the ballplayers
the Yankees
with happy laughing voices
talking about *him,*
their hero,
Big Dago.

SAYING IT OUT LOUD

It was obvious, of course,
even though
I had never said it
out loud
before.
I thought about it
all the time:
in the shed
on the sandlot
in school
at church
in the visiting room
      on the other side
      of the bars
      waiting to see
      my father
even then,
I thought about it.
But I saved it for
a day

when the cheering
on the radio
was particularly loud
and I knew it was
the right time
to say it out loud:

> I want to be
> Joe DiMaggio
> when I grow up.

>> *That's wonderful,*
>> Papa-Angelo said,
>> *but someone else*
>> *already is.*

SILENCE

Papa-Angelo never said anything
directly
about that father of mine.
No, he never said much
at all
but would stuff
my pockets
with ripe tomatoes and peppers
so his daughter
could stretch the sauce
enough to last
one more day,
which was something
he never imagined
he'd be doing
in America.

HOLIDAYS

My sisters and I
always loved
Christmas and Easter
and even Thanksgiving,
like all good
American boys and girls.
We loved
the celebrations
at school
and the songs
and the special food
Mama placed on the table
as if by magic.

My father, I think,
loved holidays, too,
somehow
always had
high expectations
of perfection,
always seemed
to enjoy
making memories.
"You'll never forget
this Christmas!"
he had a way
of announcing
just before his fist
crashed
into someone's face.

THE STREAK

It seems like
the perfect number, now,
56
like it was always
meant to be,
fifty-six parts equals
one whole.

For another long summer
each game
was its own world,
a world that
triumphed and survived
every time Joe DiMaggio's
foot safely touched
first base.

Hits were the same as
hope
that summer,

filling our hearts
in the face of
the truth
that the president
had been wrong:
there really was
something to fear
after all.

It seems like
the perfect number, now,
56
but at the time
we prayed
with all our might that
the streak
would go on
forever.

BROKEN HEARTS

Papa-Angelo liked to look at
newspaper photographs
of Joe DiMaggio's parents,
old people like him
who had been young
in Italy once.

They were always
smiling,
the DiMaggios,
always had a hand
on their son's shoulder,
proud people
with sad eyes,
smiling in America.

Papa-Angelo studied
the photographs
of Joe and his parents,
smiled himself, and
shook his head
at the wonder of
it all.

> *Look how he has made*
> *their broken hearts soar.*

WAR

Bombs fell
on Pearl Harbor
and my father
was released before
his sentence was over
and all the
newspapers
showed Joe DiMaggio
looking uncomfortable
in a uniform
not meant for
playing baseball.

War
was all
everyone talked about
except for Papa-Angelo
who almost
stopped talking
altogether.

HOME FRONT

My father said
many times
that there was
important work
to be done
on the home front, too;
not everyone
had to go
to war.

The country needed
strong men
at home
in the factories,
pounding scrap metal
into sheets,
doing their part
for the war effort.

He smiled
when he said
these things
and I was supposed
to believe that
somewhere else
in America
there was
another
convicted felon
on the home front,
working a factory job
and lying to his son,
another strong man
who walked down
busy streets
with his head held high,
faking a limp
for the war effort.

HANDS

Papa-Angelo never said much
about the letters and packages
of clothes and food
he sent every week
to the relatives
in Italy.

He said even less
after the old village
was occupied
by Germans
and the letters
came back,
returned to sender,
but not the packages, of course;
someone would always want those.

I saw the thin red line
Papa-Angelo's lips became
and I saw the way his hands
shook
when he stuffed those letters
into his jacket pocket,
some almost every week
the first summer
of my life
that Joe DiMaggio
did not play baseball.

THE LONGEST BLAST

I had heard many
long blasts
before—
deep to center field
deep to left field and right,
out of the park,
the ball game is over.
But those
long blasts
were always followed by
the sound of people
cheering, clapping,
stomping their feet,
the sound of victory.

What did this blast sound like?
V-J Day, people called it,
Victory Over Japan,
the war is over.

I couldn't imagine
anyone cheering
in Hiroshima.

MY FATHER, RUNNING — 1945

Jerry DiLuca from down the street
said he saw
my father running,
running and jumping
over a backyard fence,
"A pretty good jump," he said,
"good athletes must run
in the family."

The two guys running behind
my father
didn't jump that fence
nearly as cleanly;
maybe their nightsticks
got in the way.

Jerry kept on talking
but I stopped listening,
figuring that just when
everybody else's
daddies
would be coming home
like heroes
mine would be
going away
again.

FAST

It wasn't important, really,
I knew,
but in the
upside-down, swirling
world around me
it sometimes felt good
to get out
on the sidewalks
on the streets
in the alleys
and just run,
run straight
and run fast,
streaking across the outfield
flying around the bases
making every catch,
safe every time.

Hey, Joltin' Joe,
think you're as fast
as me?

WELCOME HOME

It wasn't necessary
of course,
it wasn't anything
he had to do,
but Joe DiMaggio
hit a two-run homer
in the sixth inning
of his first game back
from the war
and Papa-Angelo and I
both let out
a sigh of relief
so pure and loud
you would have thought
the whole world
had finally remembered
how to breathe.

SMART

I won't be going
to seventh grade
next year,
I said, looking
for a reaction
and getting one.

Papa-Angelo
shot up
out of his chair
fast,
fast for an
old man,
fast for him.

And just where
will you be going
instead?

I could not bear
the sorrow
in his eyes,
could not bear
how the joke fell
flat.

　　　　To high school,
　　　　I said,
　　　　my voice small,
　　　　a whisper.

I was twelve years old,
too old
to be picked up
by an old man.

　　　　People say I'm smart,
　　　　I said softly
　　　　while my grandfather held me
　　　　and kissed the top
　　　　of my head
　　　　over and over
　　　　forever.

MISSING

"You were always
missing,"
my sister said,
surprising me.
"Were you in
that shed
listening to games,
in the library,
on the sandlot?

"Where were you
when things started
flying
around the house,
dishes and lamps,
fists and screams?

"Where were you
when I was
all alone,

hiding
under my bed?"
My sister shook
with the telling
of it all.

Most of the time,
I said carefully,
I was
all alone
in my room,
hiding
under *my* bed.

My sister stared
and then we
laughed
and laughed
like we had never heard
anything so funny
in all our lives.

HAPPINESS

I borrowed the book
from the library
on impulse,
drawn to the size
of the volume,
the color and detail
of the drawings.

Time passed quickly
as I turned the pages
of *Gray's Anatomy,*
lost in the wonder
of my discovery.

I did not know
how long
Mama had been standing there
in the doorway,

looking at me
with an expression
I had not seen before,
lost in the wonder
of her own discovery.

DREAMS 1951

I cried
when I heard
the news
on the radio,
off-season,
least-expected.

There had been
rumors,
true, but easily
dismissed
by Papa-Angelo
and me,
holding tight
to our world.

Joe DiMaggio said
he wanted to go out
on top,
retire in dignity
before he became

a shadow
passing unnoticed
among young men.

Papa-Angelo did not cry
of course.
He had been living
far beyond sadness
for too long.

He smiled instead
and comforted me.
> It is still a wonderful thing
> to dream of being
> Joe DiMaggio.
Someone else still is,
I said, and then
I said out loud
what I had never said
out loud before:
I want to be
a doctor someday.

I reached out
to touch
my grandfather's wet cheek.
    Papa mio, I said,
    you are the one
    who showed me how
    to pick up his glove.

BECOMING JOE DiMAGGIO

Summer comes
and Papa-Angelo and I
skip a game
to board a bus
heading to
the other side of town.

We stand together
on a hill
surrounded by
brick university buildings
and green courtyards—
tall black gates
loom before us,
shut tight now
but beckoning.

Dottore,
Papa-Angelo calls me already,
the second name
he has given me

sounding as good as
the first.

I am sixteen years old
and I will walk through
these tall, proud gates
in September
and someday,
I will be a doctor.

We stand there
on the hill,
my grandfather and I,
knowing who we are,
who we have become.

*Look how we have made
our broken hearts soar.*

A NOTE FROM THE AUTHOR

My father was not a storyteller. Our family was not the kind that sat on the front porch sipping lemonade and listening to the elders reminisce. We were doers and did not spend a lot of time on verbal reflection.

At the end of each day, my father came home with a smile on his lips but a furrow in his brow. As I grew older, I eventually pieced together what my father did and why he looked that way. He was a surgeon, and that is how I knew him: a man who took great joy in being with his family but was never free from the awesome concern and responsibility for his patients.

Sometime, without remembering when, exactly, I also learned about my father's life before me, before Vietnam, before medical school. Maybe it was in the car, out in the yard playing catch or pulling weeds, at the dinner table, or between the innings of a Yankees game on television. Somehow, without remembering how, exactly, I learned about a radio, a garden, a grandfather, and Joe DiMaggio.

Maybe my father was a storyteller after all.

Also by Deb Caletti

The Queen of Everything

Honey, Baby, Sweetheart